MADAGASCAR™

It's A Zoo In Here!

By Michael Anthony Steele

DREAMWORKS
ANIMATION SKG

Scholastic Inc.

New York   Toronto   London   Auckland   Sydney
Mexico City   New Delhi   Hong Kong   Buenos Aires

ISBN: 0-439-78585-5

Madagascar TM & © 2005 DreamWorks Animation L.L.C.

Published by Scholastic Inc.
SCHOLASTIC and associated logos are trademarks and/or registered trademarks of Scholastic Inc.

12 11 10 9 8 7 6 5 4 3 2 1   5 6 7 8 9 10/0

Designed by Joseph Williams
Printed in the U.S.A.
First printing, May 2005

t was another beautiful morning at the City Zoo. The clock chimed 10:00 and the gates swung open. A flood of people poured in to see the star of the zoo — Alex the lion.

Alex couldn't wait to perform for the people. "Let's go!" he yelled to the other animals. "It's showtime!"

The chimpanzees, Phil and Mason, were just waking up over coffee and donuts.

On the other hand, the penguins had been up for hours. They waddled in their pen, looking cute and cuddly.

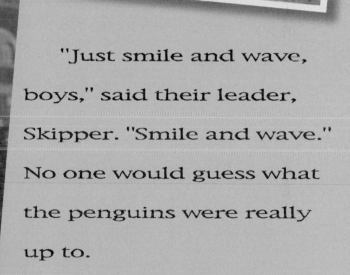

"Just smile and wave, boys," said their leader, Skipper. "Smile and wave." No one would guess what the penguins were really up to.

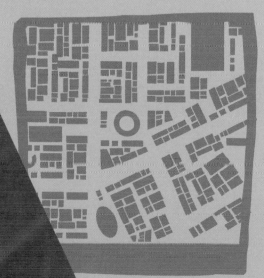

"We're open!" Alex yelled to his three best friends. "It's another fabulous day!"

Marty the zebra began to stretch and warm up. "Going to try something new today," he declared. "Going to keep it fresh!"

Gloria the hippo slowly emerged from her pool and looked at Alex. "I need ten more minutes of sleep," she said groggily and sank back down.

Melman the giraffe poked his head out of his shed. "I'm calling in sick," he announced.

"**G**ather round, people!" Marty shouted. "Big zebra show about to start!"

Marty danced around his pen and squirted water out of his mouth. Children giggled loudly as he shoved one hoof under his arm and made rude armpit noises.

Marty laughed. "You won't see that on television!"

ROOOOOOARRR!!!

Alex's act was as spectacular as ever. Confetti floated down and fireworks boomed as he prowled and posed in front of the spectators. He took a deep breath, then let out his famous, thunderous ROOOOOOOOAAAAAAAAR!

As usual, the crowd went wild.

"Thanks for coming, folks!" Marty said as his audience moved on. "I hope you thought that was fresh."

Suddenly, a hole opened in the ground. Marty peered closer as four penguins poked their heads out. They were surprised to see Marty.

"What are you guys doing?" asked Marty.

"We're digging to Antarctica!" said Skipper.

"Ant-hootica?" asked Marty.

"We don't belong here," Skipper explained. "We're going to the wide-open spaces of Antarctica. To the wild!"

Marty's eyes widened.

That night, after the zoo had closed, the animals were served tasty food. Then they were pampered and spoiled with everything an animal could want.

Gloria sighed as she enjoyed a massage. "This is the life."

Melman was offered a wide assortment of vitamins. "I'm in heaven," he moaned.

Marty had his hooves polished, and Alex's mane was styled. Then they both settled down to dinner. Marty had Kentucky blue grass, while Alex had steak.

After dinner, Alex, Gloria, and Melman had a birthday party for Marty. There were presents and a cake with a great big birthday candle.

"Let's go," said Gloria. "Make a wish, babycakes!"

Marty closed his eyes and blew out the candle.

"What did you wish for?" asked Alex.

"I wished that I could go to the wild!" said Marty.

"The wild?" asked Alex. "Are you nuts? That's crazy!"

"The penguins are going," said Marty. "So why can't I?"

"The penguins are psychotic!" replied Alex.

Marty sighed.

Later that night, when all the animals were asleep, Melman poked his head into Alex's pen. "Alex," he whispered.

Alex opened his eyes. Embarrassed, he jerked his thumb from his mouth. "What is it, Melman?"

"It's Marty," replied the giraffe. "He's gone!"

Gloria was so worried about Marty that she burst through the zoo wall. Melman and Alex followed. Then, the three friends hurried off to find Marty.

Meanwhile, Marty was having the time of his life! He ran through the park, he strutted down the sidewalks, and he glided across an ice rink. Then, he went to find the train station so he could catch a train into the wild.

Alex, Gloria, and Melman found Marty at the train station. Alex flew through the air and tackled the zebra. "I've got him! I've got him!"

"He's got him!" yelled Gloria.

"He's got him!" repeated Melman as he crashed his head into a large clock. The clumsy giraffe staggered across the floor with the clock stuck firmly on his head. "I'm okay," he said in a muffled voice.

"What are you guys doing here?" asked Marty.

Alex shook Marty by the shoulders. "Don't you ever do this again! Do you hear me?"

Suddenly, the friends looked up and saw that they were surrounded by police officers. Alex tried to explain, but all the police heard was a fierce roar.

On a nearby bench, a group of penguins gazed at the police. "We've been ratted out, boys," said Skipper as the penguins raised their flippers.

The next morning, the animals woke to find themselves inside four crates aboard a large cargo ship.

"What's going on?" asked Gloria.

"We're getting transferred!" Alex shouted.

In another crate, Skipper poked his head out of an airhole. He glanced at a nearby chimpanzee cage. "You!" he yelled. "Can you read?"

Phil squinted at the writing on the crate. Then he turned and gestured to Mason. "Hmm," said Mason. He turned to the penguins. "It says, 'Ship to Kenya Wildlife Preserve, Africa.'"

"Africa?" yelped Skipper. "That's not going to fly!"

A penguin named Rico coughed up a paper clip and carefully picked the lock. The group of birds slipped out of their crate and quietly waddled toward the ship's bridge.

Cautiously, they snuck onto the bridge and up behind the ship's captain.

WHAP!

They knocked him out with a well-placed karate chop.

"Let's get this tin can turned around," announced Skipper.

As the ship turned, the crates holding Alex, Marty, Gloria, and Melman broke free. They fell overboard and bobbed up and down in the churning ocean. Luckily, the crates washed ashore on a nearby island. The four friends found themselves on a long deserted beach.

"Oh, look at us," Gloria said with a smile. "We're all here together, safe and sound!"

"Yeah, here we are," Melman agreed. "But where exactly *is* here?"

Marty gazed at the massive tropical jungle in front of them. "This sure isn't the city zoo!"

"Sssssh!" said Alex. "Do you hear that?"

There was music coming from the jungle.

"Where there's music, there's people!"

said Gloria. The four friends ran through the

jungle to find the people.

Back on the boat, the

penguins were celebrating.

They were headed to the

wild at last.

Deep in the jungle, a group of lemurs was having a party—watched by some mean-looking animals called fossa.

Alex burst into the clearing. A huge spider had landed on his shoulder and he danced around trying to get rid of it. The fossa panicked, and melted back into the jungle.

The locals watched from the bushes. "What are they?" asked Mort, a cute little lemur. "I don't know. But I have a plan," declared King Julien, and with that, he threw Mort into the clearing.

Alex bent down to talk to Mort, but he scared him instead. So Gloria picked Mort up and cradled him in her arms, cooing at him.

The other locals were so happy that Mort hadn't been eaten, that they ran out of the bushes to welcome the four New Yorkers to the wild.

Back on the beach, Marty yelled and danced. "We're in the wild! We're in the wild! This could be the best thing that's ever happened!"

Alex didn't think so. He thought that it was the worst thing that had ever happened, and he was fed up with Marty. Alex drew a line in the sand. "This is your side of the island and this side of the island is for me, Gloria, and Melman," he told the zebra.

"Fine," said Marty. "If you need me, I'll be on the fun side of the island."

Meanwhile, the penguins had finally reached Antarctica—and they didn't like it. It was cold . . . *very* cold. So they headed back to the ship to look for someplace warm.

In the wild, Alex tried to build a rescue beacon, but Melman destroyed it. Then he made a rescue sign. That didn't work either. Marty, however, was having a great time in the wild. His jungle home was perfect.

lex decided to join Marty on the fun side of the island, but first he had to apologize.

"I've been thinking about what you said. If this is what you want then I'll give it a shot," he said to Marty.

The four friends spent the rest of the evening sitting around the fire in Marty's hut, eating seaweed on a stick, and gazing at the stars.

On another part of the island, King Julien was explaining his plan to keep the new arrivals happy. . . .

The next morning, when the four friends awoke, they were in paradise.

Marty and Alex took off running, chasing each other and having fun, but something strange happened. Alex started feeling—and acting—wild . . . *very* wild!

Alex was banished to the dangerous fossa side of the island.

Braaaap! The boat and the penguins appeared offshore. Gloria and Melman ran to the beach, while Marty went looking for Alex.

The hungry fossa had followed Marty and were about to pounce when Alex appeared to save his friend. But there were too many fossa.

Gloria, Melman, the locals, and the penguins all arrived to help, and the fossa were finally chased away.

Later that day, there was a big party on the beach to celebrate. The four friends realized that it didn't matter where they were so long as they were together.